Woozle the Wizard
and other scary stories

Woozle the Wizard
and other scary stories

Written by
Caroline Repchuk, Geoff Cowan and Kat Wooton

Illustrated by
Diana Catchpole, Robin Edmonds
and Chris Forsey

p

This is a Parragon book
First published in 2000

Parragon
Queen Street House
4 Queen Street
Bath BA1 1HE, UK

Produced by
The Templar Company plc,
Pippbrook Mill, London Road,
Dorking, Surrey RH4 1JE UK

Edited by Caroline Repchuk

Designed by Caroline Reeves

Printed and bound in Spain
ISBN 0 75253 405 X

Contents

Woozle the Wizard

An icy wind howled through the trees. Woozle the Wizard shivered and pulled his cloak tightly around him as he hurried along a pathway that had been cleared at the edge of the wood. Thick snow was piled high on either side of the path, and above great branches creaked and groaned beneath the weight of their snowy blankets. "Not an evening to be outside," muttered the wizard to himself, as he strode along.

But Woozle had no choice. He had promised to deliver an important potion to Mrs Bunny, to cure her babies from an attack of the measles, and he didn't want to let her down.

On his way home, the skies grew even darker, and another snowstorm began. Woozle could barely see the pathway in front of him as he struggled bravely onwards through the storm. Small wonder then, that he didn't see little Mole until it was too late. Mole was scurrying along in the other direction, heading for the warmth of his cosy hole. Then suddenly "Whoomph!", with a crash and a bang, Woozle and Mole collided, sending each other flying! Mole landed upside down in a bank of snow, and Woozle had to pull him out. While Mole felt about in the snow for his glasses, Woozle straightened out the point of his crumpled hat. Then after checking that no-one was hurt, they each continued on their way.

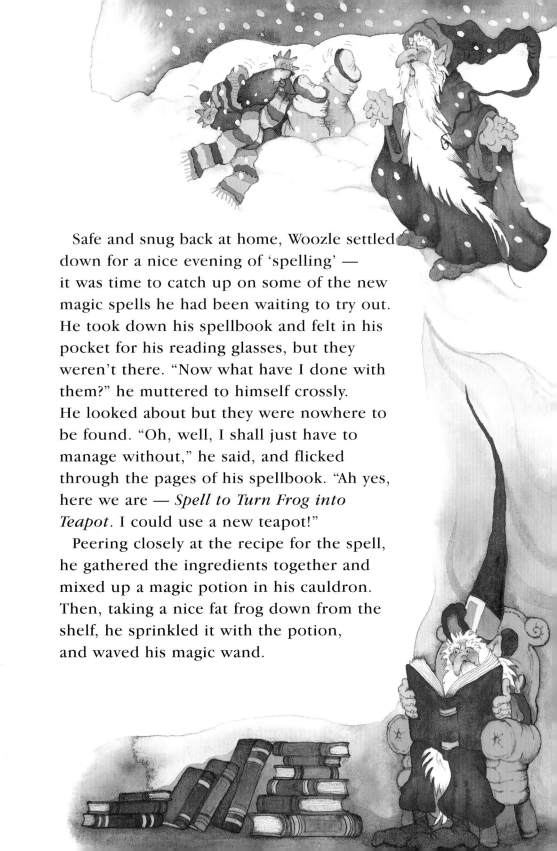

Safe and snug back at home, Woozle settled
down for a nice evening of 'spelling' —
it was time to catch up on some of the new
magic spells he had been waiting to try out.
He took down his spellbook and felt in his
pocket for his reading glasses, but they
weren't there. "Now what have I done with
them?" he muttered to himself crossly.
He looked about but they were nowhere to
be found. "Oh, well, I shall just have to
manage without," he said, and flicked
through the pages of his spellbook. "Ah yes,
here we are — *Spell to Turn Frog into
Teapot*. I could use a new teapot!"

Peering closely at the recipe for the spell,
he gathered the ingredients together and
mixed up a magic potion in his cauldron.
Then, taking a nice fat frog down from the
shelf, he sprinkled it with the potion,
and waved his magic wand.

"Make me a shiny little teapot," cried the wizard. With a crackle and fizz, the frog disappeared and there in its place stood a tiny metal robot.

"Oh, dear," said Woozle. "I must have misread something. Still, a robot could be useful. Go and wait in the corner," he told it, and the little robot did as it was told.

Woozle tried another spell. "This looks simple enough — *Slug into Bowl of Fruit*. Very tasty." But this time when he waved his wand a mug inside a rubber boot appeared. "Well, that's no use at all," sighed Woozle.

He tried to turn a snail into hot buttered toast, but instead he got a fat little ghost, and in place of a chocolate cake he got a garden rake.

"It's no use, I give up," Woozle sighed. He sat back in his favourite armchair and closed his eyes to think. Where had he put his glasses?

Just then he heard a faint scraping at the door.

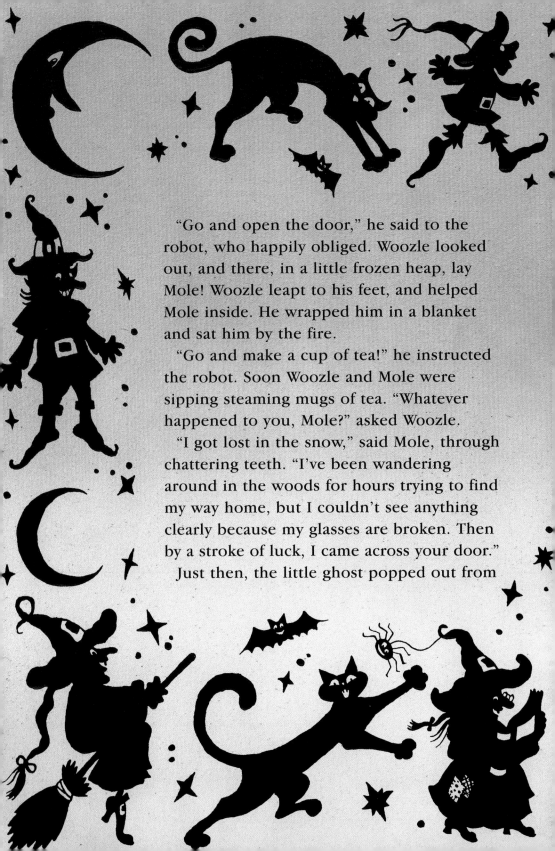

"Go and open the door," he said to the robot, who happily obliged. Woozle looked out, and there, in a little frozen heap, lay Mole! Woozle leapt to his feet, and helped Mole inside. He wrapped him in a blanket and sat him by the fire.

"Go and make a cup of tea!" he instructed the robot. Soon Woozle and Mole were sipping steaming mugs of tea. "Whatever happened to you, Mole?" asked Woozle.

"I got lost in the snow," said Mole, through chattering teeth. "I've been wandering around in the woods for hours trying to find my way home, but I couldn't see anything clearly because my glasses are broken. Then by a stroke of luck, I came across your door."

Just then, the little ghost popped out from

where he had been hiding behind the sofa.
Mole almost dropped his tea in fright, but
Woozle shooed the little ghost away. He told
Mole about his spells all going wrong.

"I must find my glasses, but I don't know
where else to look," said Woozle.

"Why don't you look in your crystal ball?"
asked Mole.

"Well, I would, but I need my glasses to
see in it clearly," said Woozle.

"Why don't you try mine?" said Mole
helpfully. "If we put some tape round the
middle, they should be OK!"

Woozle looked doubtful, but he perched
them on his nose, and blinked in amazement.

"Perfect!" he said. "They're as good as my
own!" He gazed into his crystal ball.

"Can you see anything?" asked Mole, excitedly.

"Yes!", said Woozle, "I can see snow swirling, and someone hurrying along a path. Oh, I can see my glasses lying in the snow! And here I am, bending down to pick them up — no, wait a minute, it's not me, it's you! I can see you, Mole. You're putting the glasses in your pocket!"

"But how can they be mine, when mine are here?" asked Mole, puzzled.

Woozle scratched his head and thought hard.

"I've got it! My glasses must have fallen out of my pocket when we bumped into each other, and you must have picked them up by mistake. Which means that your glasses are still in the snow, and my glasses are, well — they're right here on the end of my nose where they belong!" The two friends chuckled at such a mix-up!

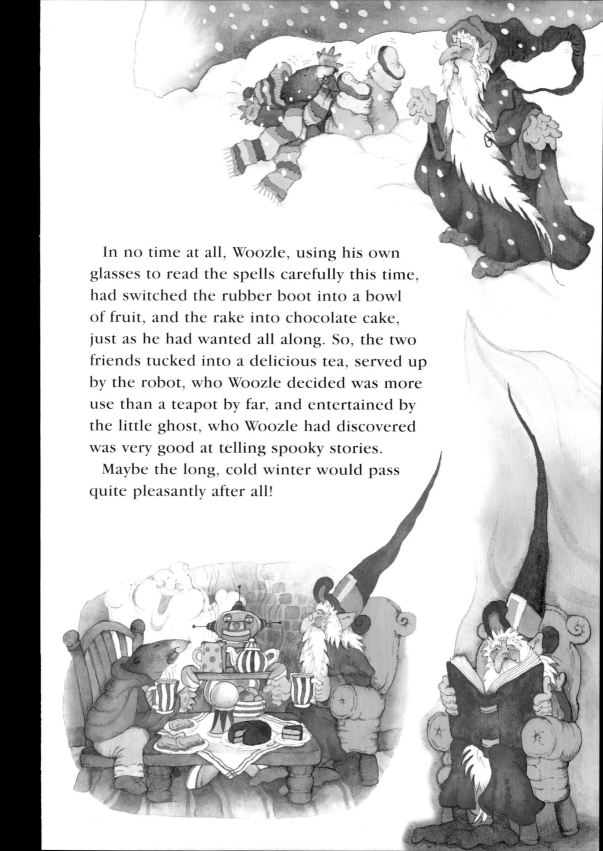

In no time at all, Woozle, using his own
glasses to read the spells carefully this time,
had switched the rubber boot into a bowl
of fruit, and the rake into chocolate cake,
just as he had wanted all along. So, the two
friends tucked into a delicious tea, served up
by the robot, who Woozle decided was more
use than a teapot by far, and entertained by
the little ghost, who Woozle had discovered
was very good at telling spooky stories.

Maybe the long, cold winter would pass
quite pleasantly after all!

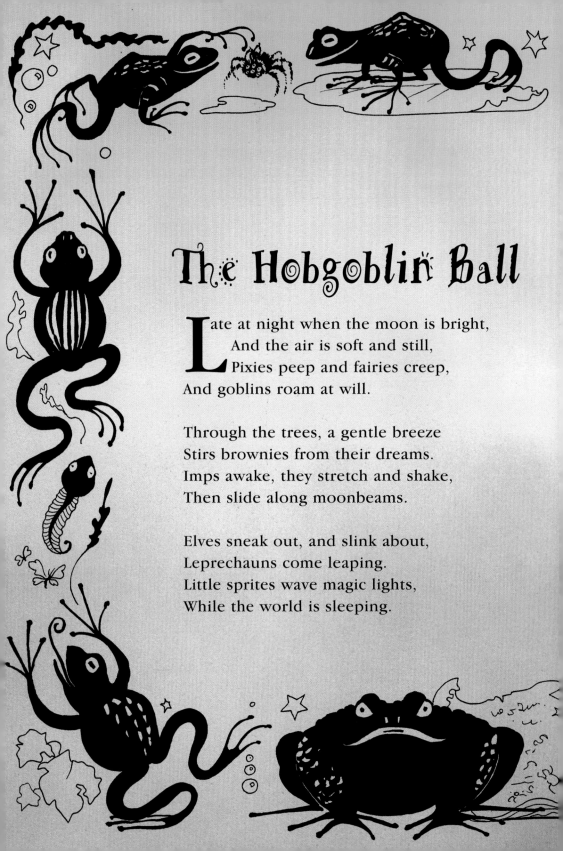

The Hobgoblin Ball

Late at night when the moon is bright,
    And the air is soft and still,
    Pixies peep and fairies creep,
And goblins roam at will.

Through the trees, a gentle breeze
Stirs brownies from their dreams.
Imps awake, they stretch and shake,
Then slide along moonbeams.

Elves sneak out, and slink about,
Leprechauns come leaping.
Little sprites wave magic lights,
While the world is sleeping.

Singing songs, they skip along,
Towards the forest glade.
Hung with lights, all twinkling bright,
While gentle music's played.

They appear, from far and near,
A host of fairy folk.
This happy band dance hand in hand,
Beneath the magic oak.

Every night, enchanting sights
Await for one and all.
So when day's done, come join the fun,
At the great Hobgoblin Ball!

The Wrong Cat

"I need three dead mice for this spell, Grazelgritch. Go and catch them," said Witch Yukspell, shoving her black cat out of the door.

Poor Grazelgritch – it was freezing cold outside and a nasty sleety rain had started. He headed for the woods and sat under a holly bush waiting for a mouse to pass by.

"Hello," said a voice behind him. "Is this a good place to catch mice?" He turned to see another black cat crouching under the holly. Grazelgritch thought she was beautiful.

"Who are you?" he asked. "I've never seen you in the woods before."

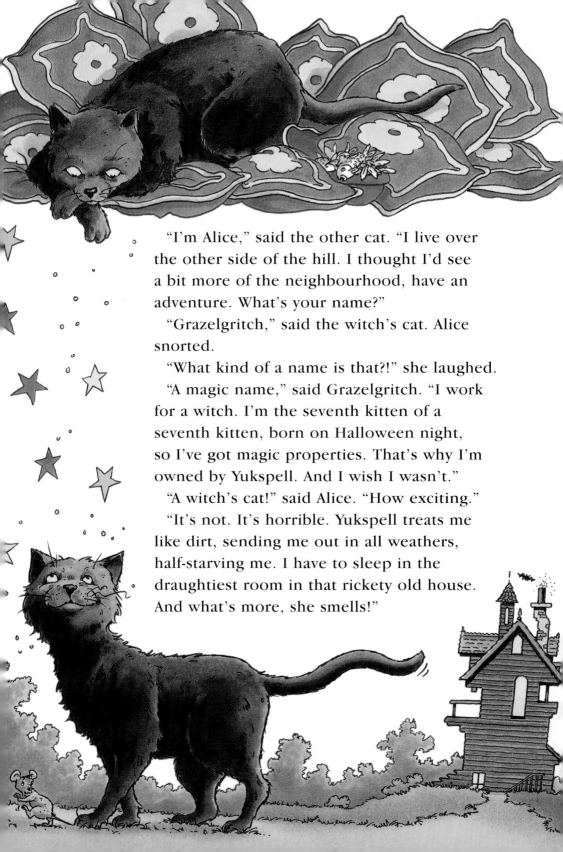

"I'm Alice," said the other cat. "I live over the other side of the hill. I thought I'd see a bit more of the neighbourhood, have an adventure. What's your name?"

"Grazelgritch," said the witch's cat. Alice snorted.

"What kind of a name is that?!" she laughed.

"A magic name," said Grazelgritch. "I work for a witch. I'm the seventh kitten of a seventh kitten, born on Halloween night, so I've got magic properties. That's why I'm owned by Yukspell. And I wish I wasn't."

"A witch's cat!" said Alice. "How exciting."

"It's not. It's horrible. Yukspell treats me like dirt, sending me out in all weathers, half-starving me. I have to sleep in the draughtiest room in that rickety old house. And what's more, she smells!"

"You poor thing," said Alice. "I lead a
very boring life – sleeping most of the day,
eating tinned food, leftovers if I'm lucky.
I have to go to the vet sometimes."

"Sounds like heaven," sighed Grazelgritch,
nibbling at a flea between his toes.

"Well, why don't we swap for a while?"
suggested Alice. "Go on – have a holiday.
And I can have my adventure!"

Grazelgritch thought she must be bonkers
but he agreed at once, and Alice took the
dead mice they caught to the witch's house
on the hill.

"About time too!" snapped Yukspell,
grabbing the mice and flinging them into the
cauldron. "You look fatter. How many mice
did you gobble up before you brought these
home, you idle, greedy, useless cat?!"

She added the ingredients to her wicked witches' brew. It was a spell to make all the local school children sick.

"Just one more thing," said Yukspell. She grabbed Alice by the scruff of her neck and wrenched out a whisker – ping! Alice yowled in pain and jumped on to the windowsill, whipping her tail back and forth. Yukspell ignored the angry cat and dropped the whisker into the cauldron. At that point the whole mixture was meant to turn green and froth violently. But it didn't.

"Funny," said the witch, checking her spell book. Of course the problem was that Alice was an ordinary cat – the fourth kitten in a litter of six, born at Easter – not a magic cat at all. Yukspell was furious. Four hours work wasted.

"Grazelgritch!" she screeched. "Were those mice or voles?!" She turned and stared at the black cat. Then slowly the truth dawned on Yukspell.

"An imposter!" she screamed. "You're not Grazelgritch!" She grabbed Alice and threw her out of the window.

"You're lucky I didn't put you in the cauldron!" she shouted after the poor cat, as Alice raced away down the hill.

When Alice got home, she found Grazelgritch purring contentedly on her owner's lap.

"Oh no! That was quick!" he said. "Do I have to go back so soon? I haven't had supper yet."

"I don't think I'd make a good adventurer," said Alice. "But it's all right, don't go. My owners said just the other day that they'd like to give a home to another cat to keep me company. Well, I choose you!"

Yukspell was furious that Grazelgritch had deserted her. Without a magic cat none of her spells worked any more, which made life a lot more pleasant for everyone else who lived around her. She had to content herself with scaring people on her broomstick.

Alice's owners were happy to give a home
to her new friend. And wouldn't you know it?
The following autumn, Alice had seven sooty
black kittens. But Grazelgritch chose the new
home for the youngest kitten very carefully –
it went to live with a very nice family in the
town. They never knew that they owned a
magical cat, and that's exactly how
Grazelgritch wanted it.

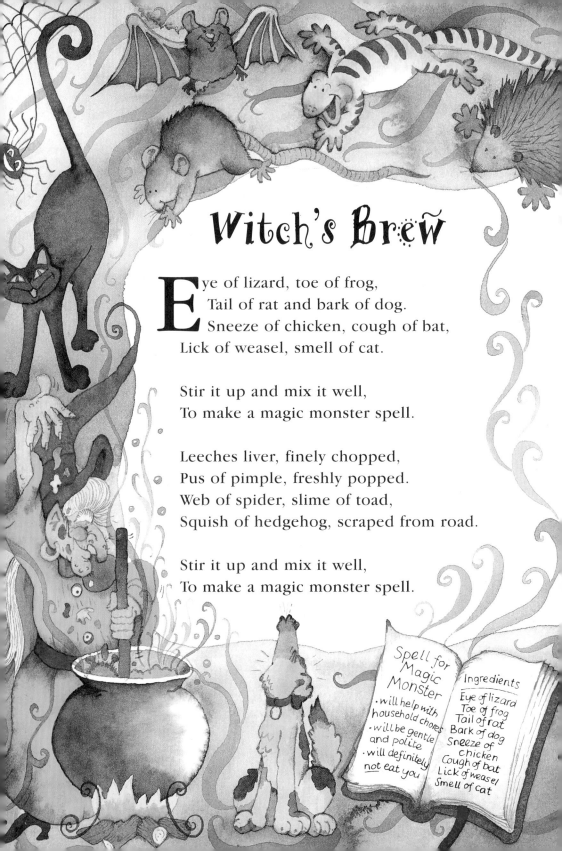

Witch's Brew

E ye of lizard, toe of frog,
   Tail of rat and bark of dog.
   Sneeze of chicken, cough of bat,
Lick of weasel, smell of cat.

Stir it up and mix it well,
To make a magic monster spell.

Leeches liver, finely chopped,
Pus of pimple, freshly popped.
Web of spider, slime of toad,
Squish of hedgehog, scraped from road.

Stir it up and mix it well,
To make a magic monster spell.

Spell for
Magic
Monster
· will help with
household chores
· will be gentle
and polite
· will definitely
not eat you

Ingredients
Eye of lizard
Toe of frog
Tail of rat
Bark of dog
Sneeze of
chicken
Cough of bat
Lick of weasel
Smell of cat

Now it's done, the spell is ready,
The monster's rising, slow and steady.
"Pleased to meet you," Witchy sighs.
"Pleased to *eat* you," he replies.

What's gone wrong, she cannot tell,
To spoil the magic monster spell.

The witch goes pale, she must act fast,
Or else this day may be her last!
She grabs her wand. She has a notion
Of how to get rid of this potion.

She shakes her wand, which breaks the spell,
And waves the monster fond farewell!

Smoky Smells Success

Smoky was a spook, and a very happy spook at that! He haunted an ancient castle, surrounded by a wide moat. From deep in its darkest dungeons to high on the heights of its battlements, Smoky would appear, mischievously and mysteriously, whenever he wanted. Sometimes, he appeared just as himself — a swirling puff of supernatural smoke. However, being a ghost, Smoky could change shape at will.

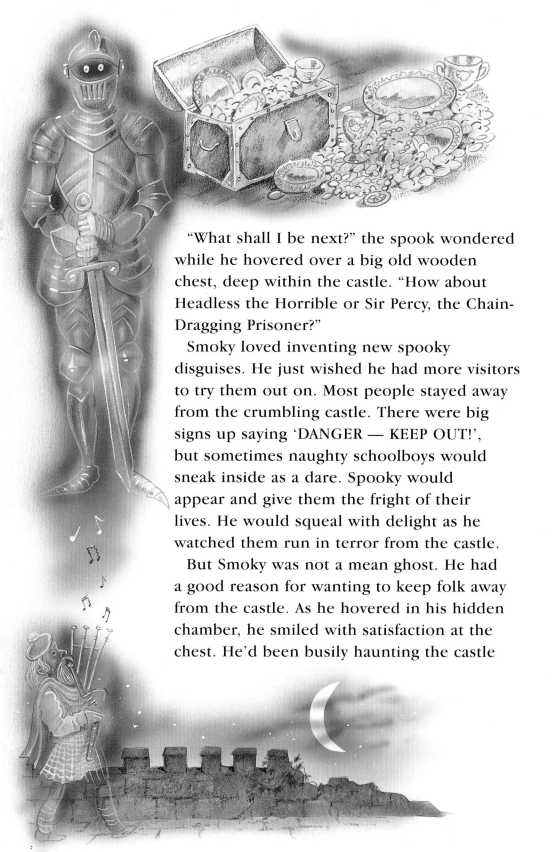

"What shall I be next?" the spook wondered while he hovered over a big old wooden chest, deep within the castle. "How about Headless the Horrible or Sir Percy, the Chain-Dragging Prisoner?"

Smoky loved inventing new spooky disguises. He just wished he had more visitors to try them out on. Most people stayed away from the crumbling castle. There were big signs up saying 'DANGER — KEEP OUT!', but sometimes naughty schoolboys would sneak inside as a dare. Spooky would appear and give them the fright of their lives. He would squeal with delight as he watched them run in terror from the castle.

But Smoky was not a mean ghost. He had a good reason for wanting to keep folk away from the castle. As he hovered in his hidden chamber, he smiled with satisfaction at the chest. He'd been busily haunting the castle

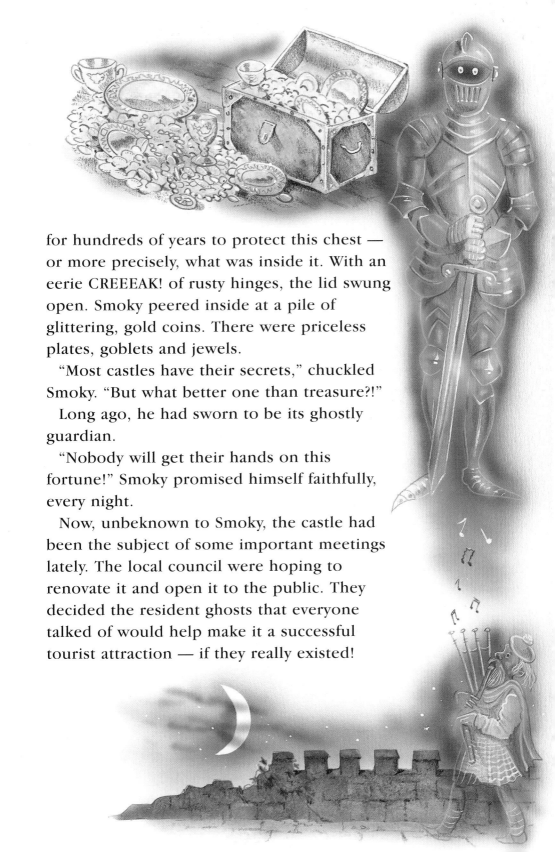

for hundreds of years to protect this chest —
or more precisely, what was inside it. With an
eerie CREEEAK! of rusty hinges, the lid swung
open. Smoky peered inside at a pile of
glittering, gold coins. There were priceless
plates, goblets and jewels.

"Most castles have their secrets," chuckled
Smoky. "But what better one than treasure?!"

Long ago, he had sworn to be its ghostly
guardian.

"Nobody will get their hands on this
fortune!" Smoky promised himself faithfully,
every night.

Now, unbeknown to Smoky, the castle had
been the subject of some important meetings
lately. The local council were hoping to
renovate it and open it to the public. They
decided the resident ghosts that everyone
talked of would help make it a successful
tourist attraction — if they really existed!

So it was that one morning, Smoky heard a car pull up. A man and woman climbed out. They walked slowly around the castle walls, making notes, and looking very serious indeed.

"It's no use," said the man. "This castle's crumbling. If we don't pull it down, it will fall all on its own. We're going to have to forget about opening it to the public."

"Pity," replied the woman. "It's such a grand, historical building. If only we could raise enough money to have it repaired. But that would cost a fortune!"

Smoky froze. For the first time, he understood what it was like to be scared! If his precious castle was pulled down, what would happen to him? He wouldn't want to haunt anywhere else. Something had to be done — and fast!

As the visitors were returning to their car, they suddenly stopped and sniffed the air. There was a wonderful smell coming from the castle. The man pointed to what looked like a thin trail of steam floating by the entrance. It was Smoky, who had conjured up a delicious smell to tempt the visitors in.

"Let's take a look inside," said the man.

"But it's dangerous — and apparently haunted!" said the woman, nervously.

"We'll be careful," said the man. "I have to find out where that incredible smell is coming from."

They followed the lovely smell into the castle. Smoky led the way, disguised as a thin trail of smoke. For once, he didn't want to frighten his visitors away! They crept quietly along the corridors, glancing nervously over their shoulders, but there were no spooks to be seen. Smoky made a secret door in one of the walls swing wide open. A narrow, cobweb-filled passage led the visitors to his hidden chamber and...the treasure chest!

When the officials saw its glittering, golden contents, they shrieked so loudly it made Smoky jump.

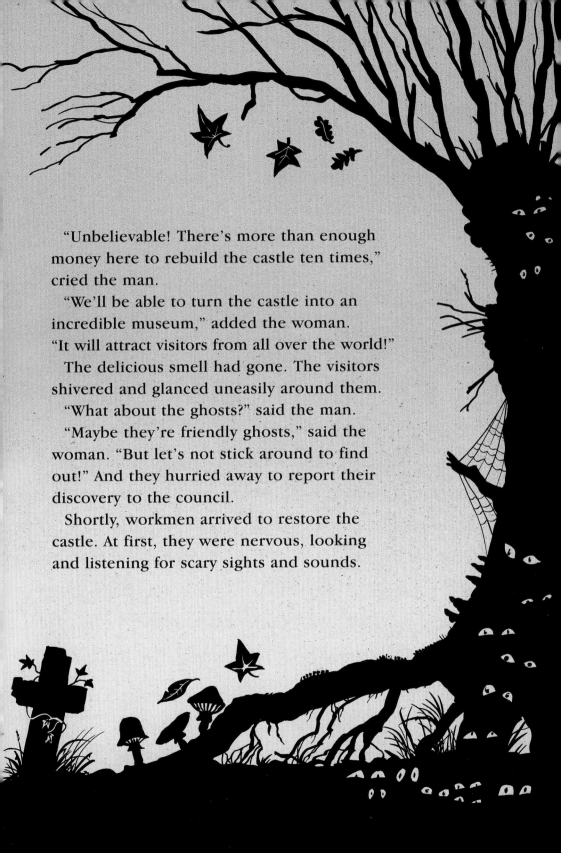

"Unbelievable! There's more than enough money here to rebuild the castle ten times," cried the man.

"We'll be able to turn the castle into an incredible museum," added the woman. "It will attract visitors from all over the world!"

The delicious smell had gone. The visitors shivered and glanced uneasily around them.

"What about the ghosts?" said the man.

"Maybe they're friendly ghosts," said the woman. "But let's not stick around to find out!" And they hurried away to report their discovery to the council.

Shortly, workmen arrived to restore the castle. At first, they were nervous, looking and listening for scary sights and sounds.

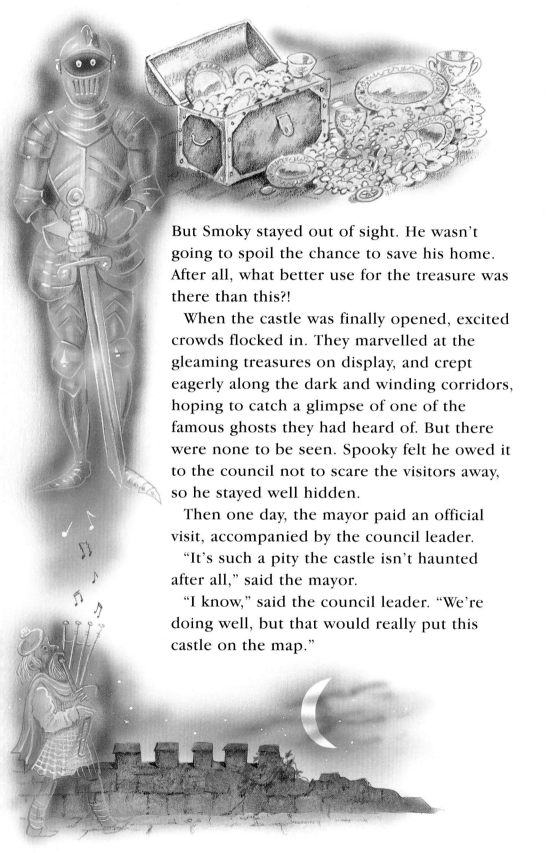

But Smoky stayed out of sight. He wasn't going to spoil the chance to save his home. After all, what better use for the treasure was there than this?!

When the castle was finally opened, excited crowds flocked in. They marvelled at the gleaming treasures on display, and crept eagerly along the dark and winding corridors, hoping to catch a glimpse of one of the famous ghosts they had heard of. But there were none to be seen. Spooky felt he owed it to the council not to scare the visitors away, so he stayed well hidden.

Then one day, the mayor paid an official visit, accompanied by the council leader.

"It's such a pity the castle isn't haunted after all," said the mayor.

"I know," said the council leader. "We're doing well, but that would really put this castle on the map."

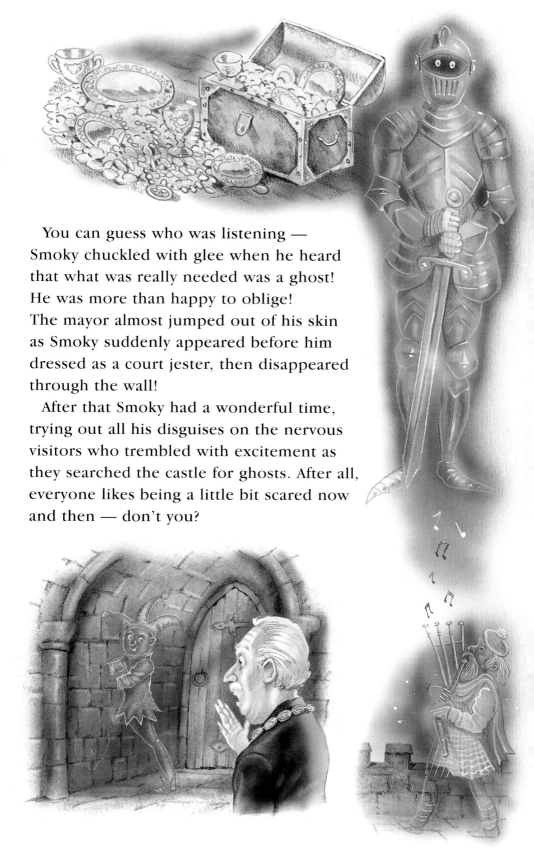

You can guess who was listening —
Smoky chuckled with glee when he heard
that what was really needed was a ghost!
He was more than happy to oblige!
The mayor almost jumped out of his skin
as Smoky suddenly appeared before him
dressed as a court jester, then disappeared
through the wall!

After that Smoky had a wonderful time,
trying out all his disguises on the nervous
visitors who trembled with excitement as
they searched the castle for ghosts. After all,
everyone likes being a little bit scared now
and then — don't you?

Creepy Castle

In a castle, dark and dusty,
Stood an armour suit all rusty.
Haunted from breastplate to visor,
Visitors were none the wiser.

Then, one day, the suit went walking,
Past some tourists who were talking.
How they stared with big, round eyes.
Some let out astonished cries!

"This way! Run!" The tour guide said,
And everybody soon had fled.
The empty suit marched down the hall,
And shut the door on one and all!

At night it used its ghostly powers,
To howl from the castle towers.
CLANK, CLANK, CLANK, it stomped around,
And made a spooky creaking sound.

Soon the news spread far and wide
And queues of tourists formed outside.
A great big crowd had come to see,
The clanking ghost that wandered free.

The empty suit was most perplexed
(And not to say a little vexed.)
He'd meant to scare them all away —
And so he left that very day!